THE CURSE OF VENNINGTON

VEDANT GARG

To mom and dad

Contents

Foreword

We tend to blindfold ourselves from the scary and creepy stuff, but if you honestly ask yourself the answer comes out to be 'Yes there is a lot of destructive evil powers to which science has no answers.' Everybody knows that there are many cursed places and people in the world who are impacted by evil spirits. So many movies have been created which are indeed based on true events in the different timeline of the world. The energy around us is half good but the other half is always scary. If there's God, there is a Devil too.

Horror stories are liked by a large number of people all around the globe, but nobody wishes to experience them in real life.

This book is the epitome of an adventurous journey that also has a connection with the horror world.

Preface

Hey there! My name is Vedant Garg, I'm a fifteen-year-old student who put up in Delhi-NCR. Being a voracious reader, my inspiration for writing comes from the famous author Ruskin Bond. For me, a day is not completed until I read or write and express my imagination in black and white for curious readers like you.

One calm night, when I was sleeping I had a horrible dream. You can call it a nightmare too! the thoughts troubled me to sleep again in peace for days after. So I decided to frame a story mentioning all of my fears, that's how I started writing this story. I always wanted to write a book with my name printed on it, it gives me immense pleasure and motivation to see my dream come true.

In fact, due to Covid-19 when the world is facing such a deadly pandemic and lockdown has been imposed everywhere and nobody knows how to make the best utilization of their spare time. It cracked into my mind to write this first novel of mine, for which I was longing for years.

This story doesn't have many illustrations because I want the words of the story itself to evoke imagination in the reader's mind and let them imagine a character in the way they uniquely perceive it. I feel that is the magic of writing.

I hope you will like my story and if you do, you can convey your feedback to me by writing at vedantgarg2005@gmail.com, I would love to get your feedback to improve myself as a storyteller!

Acknowledgements

I thank my mother, Anupma Garg, and father, Rajul Garg for always showering their love and blessings for everything in my life. Supporting me, always being there for me, believing in me, and encouraging me in all my endeavors.

My thanks to all the readers who are reading this book, people who have helped to create it, and Lastly, I thank life and its unseen spirits for the inspiration to write this story in its own unique and incredible ways.

Prologue

I am Jake, a reserved but adventure-loving boy, but what would I do when my parents become the victims of the devil's demonic intentions? Will I be able to defeat the evil spirits in time? What if the scary creatures never turn back into humans? Will I survive the horror adventures? Would I be able to become the savior of the entire town? And ultimately, will I return alive?

CHAPTER ONE

THE BEGINNING

I still can't get over what I saw that night! the night which wrecked our happy lives, the dreadful night that should never come back.

It all started in the year 1969, We lived in Vennington town. It was well-known for its historical monuments and aesthetic museums. It also had some of the most famous archaic Churches in the world. Tourists from all over the world traveled to Vennington because of its fascinating past stories and ancient identity. It wasn't a big town geographically, but still, it was densely populated and surrounded by thick forest. Being a tourist place it had a very lively and festive atmosphere. Frequently there used to be Carnivals and Concerts organized all over the town. Every house there was designed with the same architecture, We too had a duplex villa like everyone else out there.

We felt very lucky to live in a conventional town that was full of opportunities. Although, some people believed that the town was cursed and was home to evil spirits but nobody cared.

I, Jake, along with my twin sister Larra went to Harvard high school, which was located on Kelvin Clugston street beside St. Peter's Church. My classmates used to call me 'doofus' because of my shy and introvert nature but I really didn't care.

Our dad was a tourist guide earlier but then he had decided to do something in addition to that and now he's really delighted as his new business of antiques started flourishing and made a huge profit last year.

Now, every weekend we used to spend our evenings at the club in the town hall. I used to go swimming with Larra, Mom liked going to the spa and dad would get busy playing pool with his mates.

Mom was really fond of gardening, she grew potatoes, chilies, tomatoes, and what not. we also had a small backyard pond in which we had many varieties of fishes like piranhas, goldfish, and clownfish along with two turtles, four seahorses, and a toad. Mom also used to take care of my best friend, Jordy the dog.

Well, for me he wasn't just a dog! he was the source of happiness for me, without him my life seemed to be incomplete.

Whenever I felt low or discouraged, Jordy was always there for me. He would not stop licking my face until I became happy and playful. I used to take him for a walk or sometimes for fishing. It always boosted my mood to spend quality time with him. I clearly remember how Jordy would catch a catfish from the lake and get it stuck in his throat, it troubled him until I gave him a pat on his back as an act of appreciation and of course to help him swallow that damn catfish.

In recent days, we had made so many unforgettable memories in Vennengton that we had never experienced before. But it didn't last for long, there were spine-chilling events waiting for us in the timeline of our lives.

As days passed, our lives became uncanny. Whenever we tried to go out of town we just couldn't! something or the other always postponed or canceled our trips. Like, when we planned to go camping near the river which was outside the town, firstly, our car didn't start easily and when we were about to get out of the town, we had a road accident with a madman who was drunk and out of his senses. After that, we decided to go to the mountains a week after, the only bridge which was there to get out of the town was seized by the cops as someone was murdered there the night before. Likewise, other things were also topsy-turvy in our lives. After that dad didn't get time to take us on any trip or vacation.

The next month we decided to visit the Church, but when we reached there we found that the priest had been acting crazy and was only muttering one line "Everyone would be transformed, nobody would be spared!" It looked as if he was possessed by someone and was being used as a messenger.

What was he talking about? I wondered.

I kept thinking about it for days but then I came to a conclusion that it was just a pre-conceived notion and everything he said was without any essence of truth. Even my father didn't give damn importance to whatever the priest said.

Soon came my favorite festival, Christmas. It was the 25th of December 1969, we had bought a gigantic Christmas tree from the carnival. We placed it in the middle of our lawn. It took me and Larra hours to decorate it properly because of its huge and wide structure. A thought troubled me the entire day, 'What would be our presents for this year?" I thought to myself.

It was evening, Mom called us inside, the moment for which we were eagerly waiting for, to receive our presents. My Mother revealed, "This year, your father and I have divided the choices, I chose a present for Larra and your dad chose a present for you, Jake" I got disappointed, I could make out what will my father give me. Autobiographies, Poetry, Encyclopedia, or a kind of book. But my mother would give Larra something related to fashion or something cool. Larra was jumping in joy while I was sitting low-spirited. It was time to declare the presents. My mom had gifted a gold pendant and a fancy watch to Larra which seemed expensive. "What's my present dad?" I asked low-heartedly. "Is it a biography or a poetry book?" I murmured.

"No son, this time I have a unique present for you. Here it is.." he took a small wooden box from his pocket and handed over it to me. It seemed as if it was an antique wooden box. I opened it suspiciously, **it was a spiritual locket!** "What kind of a present is this!" I cried. "It will protect you from all the negative energies son, it belonged to your grandfather. there must be a reason why he only wanted you to take it, did you know he was a Precognist! I said, "It's useless! I don't believe in this stupid stuff. I threw it on the ground and went straight to my room and locked it.

I knew I didn't do right but it wasn't my fault, every year Larra would get fancy gifts and I would get all the boring things like books and now an old pendant. It was a false belief that the negative energies will go by coming near the person wearing the locket.

My dad knocked on the door and apologized, "Son, I didn't want to hurt your feelings. I just want you to be safe, what if for some reason you are alone and we aren't with you? who will keep you safe?" He made me emotional, I unlocked the door, hugged him and I too apologized "I am sorry dad, I shouldn't have reacted like that, It's just that Larra is always given fancy things and I only get books and boring stuff like that."

"Books aren't boring son! they are the ultimate source of wisdom and guidance. Only books can make you successful in life and can guide you in every situation that you have never even thought of " he tried to explain. I acted as if I was convinced, I took the present and tied it to my neck. I thanked my dad for his love and care for me.

After wearing the locket, I don't know how but I managed to sleep well from that night onwards which I wasn't able to for many nights because I had been seeing some horrible nightmares every night because of which I couldn't even sleep quite well. But now the nightmares didn't occur, It gave me a sigh of relief whenever the locket was tied to my neck. It seemed like, it could really keep the bad vibes and energies away. Maybe there was a reason why my grandfather only kept it for me.

CHAPTER TWO

THE NEW YEAR EVE

Soon came new year's eve! we were about to enter the year 1970. All the people of the town were gathered near the town hall but I alone was sitting in the house doing my assignment because I didn't like going to gatherings or heavy-crowded places. After all, I had agoraphobia.

Another reason I didn't want to go was that every year, they performed a play which was based on the past story of this town, everyone knew it except for me. I didn't like stories or plays so I was never keen to know about it.

I took some cookies and milk from the refrigerator and went to my desk. I wasn't able to focus on my work because of loud music and noise, I kept staring at the town hall which was partially visible from my window. "How do people even breathe in so much crowd!" I wondered. After some time when I had finished my meal, I got up from my rocking chair but as soon as I could turn around, suddenly a dull purple and a bright azure light drew my attention blazing through the woods. At first, the purple light wasn't so bright but with time, it kept increasing its intensity and the azure light kept diminishing simultaneously. Then the purple light ray started moving up high into the sky just like a rocket. Then after some time it split into fragments and formed some kind of a mist and it eventually spread all over the town hall area but it couldn't covered our villa.

I had never seen such a bright light of that intensity before! I wondered if I should go and check, but I didn't because it was quite perilous to go into the woods at night. Wild animals like Snakes, Bats, poisonous insects, and wasps wandered there every time.

Then later, after imagining many possibilities I came to a conclusion that maybe it's a new kind of cracker which becomes mist after getting burst.

It turned 12 AM and we entered the year 1970, A huge celebration was going in the town hall and I was celebrating alone.

Literally, every single person in the town was at the town hall except for me! I only had my best friend Jordy with me, we both celebrated the new year together by playing games like hide n seek and treasure hunting.

I played some Michael Jackson's songs, we started enjoying the moment, we had almost broken Larra's bed by jumping on its bouncy surface while eating snacks. We have had every single one in the house!

After some time were tired and Jordy slept beside me. I was also very sleepy but I waited for mom, dad, and Larra to come back home and wish them. As I was thinking this, I heard the door getting unlocked.

I ran to greet them. I hugged them tightly and wished "HAPPY NEW YEAR!" but I didn't receive in reply what I expected, they were all reactionless and with pale faces went to their respective rooms without uttering anything.

I and Larra shared a single room so I went to see her and ask her what had happened to them, but when I reached the room I found her asleep. I was confused by their behavior, I thought that maybe they all were so tired that they just want to sleep.

I went near the window to see the town hall once again, but it was all dark there! In just a matter of minutes, the whole celebration got ended. So I decided to sleep and talk to them in the morning.

it was a very weird night! I could hear wolves howling for the first time in Vennington. After an hour of unconscious sleep, I heard Jordy barking abruptly. He started barking so vigrously that I woke up and then I couldn't believe what my eyes made me see that day! my eyes were filled with horror. "Aahh!" I screamed in terror.

That scene was pure hell!

My mom, dad, and Larra all had been turning into mysterious creatures which seemed way too scary. My mom and dad were slowly becoming a vampire! their canines grew triple the size of an average human's. their nails were an inch longer than mine and their body became very veiny, it looked like they had black blood flowing in them. It looked as if they were possessed by some sort of evil powers. I looked at Larra, she was slowly turning into a werewolf! Her eyes were becoming bigger and dark red with anger.

I was completely shaken, I felt like I wasn't alive or I was into another world of vampires and werewolves! I didn't know what to do! I was crying hard, I couldn't bear seeing my loved ones in this horrible and pathetic condition, I had to go out to a safe place, I couldn't let myself to be one of those.

They started coming near me with those angry faces, I closed my eyes in fear but then after a moment I realized that they weren't able to come closer, felt like a strong magical force stopped them from doing so, I looked at my pendent, it was immensely shining. I felt thankful to my

Grandfather and without wasting a second, quickly took my backpack and gathered all the things which seemed useful from my room.

I had kept a rope, a flashlight, clothes, some snacks, an empty glass bottle, and a pistol of my father which he had kept for self-defense. I took Jordy in my arms and jumped off the window.

*I landed on my knees, "Ouchh!" I cried. I somehow lifted myself and started moving to the town hall to hide, but it became even worse when I reached the town hall. the **ENTIRE TOWN WAS CONVERTED INTO CREATURES!** and they seemed to be inclined to kill me, a human.*

They started running towards me with those hungry faces, I quickly ran towards the woods as it was the only safe place I could think of in this situation. They all were chasing us, I ran towards the woods as fast as I could. The way was very dark, street lights had stopped working. The eyes of those werewolves were glowing like shiny red rubies. Which enabled night vision in them, they were easily able to spot us in so much dark where I could not even see an inch properly. I followed Jordy as he too could see in the dark being a dog. Somehow we managed to escape from their vision, we had found a peach tree that was quite bushy and huge. I quickly kept Jordy in my open backpack and started climbing the tree with the help of the rope I had bought. It took all my efforts to climb along the rope as I was shaking so much that I could barely stay calm. Somehow, I managed to get up to the nearest branch and I sat there and took Jordy and the backpack in my arms.

I was freezing as it was the winter season and cold winds were blowing through my soul. After a few hours when the werewolves had gone off, I took out some snacks from the backpack. I just ate some and gave the rest to Jordy, I wasn't in a state to eat something. The scary faces of my family kept haunting me whenever I closed my eyes. I kept staring at my locket the entire night thinking why my grandfather left the locket only for me? did he know what was about to happen to his grandson? Could he really see the future!

As I was examining the locket closely, I discovered that it could be opened! I gently opened it, it was divided into two halves. On the left side, it had a black and white picture of my Grandfather and on the right side, it had a small note which was forcefully folded six or seven times. I opened the note, it said:

MY DEAR GRANDSON,

I KNOW THAT YOU ARE OPENING THIS PENDANT WITH TEARS IN YOUR EYES.

I ESPECIALLY LEFT THIS LOCKET FOR YOU,

AS YOU WILL EXPERIENCE WHAT I HAD TOO.

- GEORGE HARRIS

what does that mean? I thought in my mind. I had so many questions in my mind that it was impossible not to think about them and stay calm.

What did my Grandfather experience? How did he know I was about to experience something which he had experienced too? How did he know that I would have tears in my eyes while opening the locket?

Ughh, I just can't forget these perplexing questions! I couldn't sleep the whole night.

I took some peaches and kept them in my backpack, I looked down and along with Jordy started coming down the peach tree. I couldn't go back, I had to find a solution to this problem! I started moving ahead in the woods with the pistol in my hand.

I again saw some werewolves who were looking for me but I managed to hide behind the trees. I leaned and with a zig-zag movement, I moved forward. I felt like a cop who was on a mission. *After some time I realized that I have not had water since last night, "I NEED WATER!"*

I needed to find a waterbody, I had never visited the woods before so I was completely clueless as to where should I go. I just kept moving deeper and deeper but didn't find water. I laid down on the green grass as I was tired and thirsty. I started feeling sleepy, which emptied my mind and allowed me to concentrate on the sorroundings.

Suddenly I heard a sound which seemed to be like a waterfall which sounds quite nearby. We followed the sound, I had to surpass many bushes to move forward. Soon we reached a grassland, there were no trees in that part of the woods. But! there was a waterfall ahead of the grassland whose sound I had been following. We ran towards the waterfall but as we moved, I saw two hyenas who were chilling there.

Wait what!!? there are hyenas in the woods! I thought there weren't any animals here apart from some deadly reptiles and some insects.

We didn't want to become their breakfast so I had to think of a plan.

I had seen some dense bushes before entering the grassland. I went back, instructed Jordy to sit on a huge flat rock quietly and then I plucked some bushes and again came back to the waterfall. I covered myself with bushes, some of them had sharp spines which injured my fingers badly. But drinking water was more important than my fingers. So I took all the bushes in my hands, and with their support, I deceived them and slowly started moving towards the waterfall. After some time I managed to reach the waterfall. I jumped behind a huge rock which was in its base.

First, I cleaned my hands as they were bleeding due to the spines. After that, I started drinking water and filled the glass bottle for Jordy. That day, I had understood the importance of little things in life which nobody actually cares about. I never thought that I would be so desperate and would bear so much pain for just the sake of drinking water. When I was done, I again covered myself in the bushes but to my surprise, the hyenas weren't there anymore. I took a sigh of relief and started walking back to the place where I had instructed Jordy to sit quietly.

But as soon as I turned back towards the woods, I saw both the hyenas were in front of me! both of them laughed (sound made by hyenas) at me, it seemed like they were calling their mates and saying 'let's have a human breakfast for a change. I took out the pistol from my pocket and shakingly pointed it towards them but in just a matter of time, four more hyenas came from behind. I was so scared to be surrounded by six hyenas I got numbed and fainted on the ground.

CHAPTER THREE

THE UNSEEN MAGIC

"AM I ALIVE?" was the first question I asked myself when I woke up. It seemed as if I was in a cave, my hand was aching, felt like it was bleeding earlier but now it had been healed by a paste. But how was it possible? "Was I not the only human in the town." I thought.

"YES! indeed you are.." said an old charismatic woman. "You are the only human left who has not been transformed by the vampire"

She was a short woman, holding a thick wooden stick in her hand whose head was like that of a dragon. Her hair was all white but she had a charm on her face that seemed alluring.
I asked, "Who are you? And how did you know what was I thinking in my mind !?"
She smiled and replied, "**I AM A WITCH!**"
I got frightened and tried to lift myself as I was on top of a flat rock, She stopped me from doing so. She clarified," You don't have to worry my dear, I am the good witch. I won't harm you.

By hearing her sympathetic tone, I took a sigh of relief.

I asked, "Where are those six hyenas who tried to make me their breakfast?"

"They all are in my control, I didn't do any harm to them as they didn't do anything wrong in trying to eat what they are made to, flesh." She said

"Do you have magical powers!?" I asked curiously.

"Yes, but not as much as the Rythom," she replied in distress

"Who is Rythom?" I asked without wasting a second.

"Don't you know the famous story of Vennington?" she surprisingly asked.

I embarrassedly said, "Ahh, No I don't, because I don't like stories and drama"

"Haven't you been to the town hall over the years?" she asked

"No, I don't go in public places or crowds because I have agoraphobia.." I insisted.

"Oh! so should I tell you what the story of this town Vennengton is?" she asked.

"Yes if it has to do something with the situation then why not," I replied.

But before you start the story, do you know where my dog Jordy is!?" I asked in distress.

"Hmm...." She thought something in her head and took out a glass ball from her pocket and chanted a mantra, "Qualfa Qualfa Geryum Yum- Qualfa Qualfa Geryum Yum" while seeing her do that, I felt like I was in a fantasy world.

After some time the transparent glass globe turned blue.

The witch told, "Your dog isn't in danger for now. This blue signal means that he is still alive and roaming around freely."

Suddenly she saw the locket on my neck.

"Where did you get this locket from!" she screamed.

"Ahh, actually my father gifted it to me on Christmas." I clarified.

"But I had given this pendant to George!" she told.

"When did you give him this pendant?" I asked.

"104 years from now, to a kid whose age was the same as yours" she remembered.

"104 YEARS!? What is your age then?" I asked.

"I have been assigned a life span till eternity until I'm summoned by the Lords!" she announced.

"Wait a minute...George? wait why is this name familiar?" I asked myself.

I took out the note of my grandfather and looked at it.

"Did you give it to George Harris?" I asked in a mysterious tone.

"YES!" she told.

"He was my Grandfather.." I told the witch.

I showed her the note and asked her "How did you know my Grandfather?"

"To understand that first you need to know the story of Vennington!" she told.

EARLIER IN THE 19TH CENTURY, THE PEOPLE OF THIS TOWN WORSHIPPED THE EVILS,

THEY BELIEVED THAT WORSHIPPING THE EVIL POWERS WILL KEEP THE TOWN SAFE.

EVERY DAY, A LIFE WAS SACRIFICED IN THE NAME OF OFFERINGS TO THE EVIL LORD.

BUT AS TIME PASSED, THEY STOPPED PRACTICING THIS RITUAL.

BUT AS THEY WORSHIPPED THE EVILS, THEY GOT WHAT THEY DESERVED!

THE EVIL LORD BECAME FURIOUS, HE SENT A DEADLY EVIL CREATURE TO DESTROY THE TOWN,

TO MAKE PEOPLE WORSHIP THEM AGAIN, AND OFFER LIVES.

THE EVIL SPIRIT TURNED ITSELF INTO A VAMPIRE,

EVERY YEAR ON THE NEW YEAR, HE TRIED TO POSSESS PEOPLE OR TURN THEM INTO EVIL CREATURES.
SO THE LORDS ALSO HAD TO SEND A POWERFUL GOOD SPIRIT TO STOP HIM.
THE GOOD SPIRIT TURNED HERSELF INTO A WITCH,
I STOPPED THE VAMPIRE EVERY YEAR WITH MY MAGICAL POWERS,
BECAUSE I WAS THE GOOD SPIRIT WHICH WAS SENT BY THE LORDS!

"But now with time, my powers have almost diminished. I tried to stop the devil once again on new year's eve but this time I failed to do so."

"WAIT WAIT WAIT WAIT...."

Now I am understanding a little, why that priest had been possessed and why did he say that everyone would be transformed.

"Do you have azure powers?" I asked.

"Yes, my powers are azure and the Devil's are bright purple in color."

"So the purple and the azure lights which came from the woods were you two battling!?"

"Yes," she replied.

I had got some answers to some of my questions but the story of my Grandfather was still a mystery.

"How did you know my Grandfather?" I asked the witch.

"He was a very sweet and innocent boy!" she smiled.

"94 years ago, George also faced what you are facing today. It was the year 1876. That year the vampire had won the battle by deception. It wasn't a fair battle!

When we defeated him, I told him that by the year 1970 the Rythom would again win as my powers would diminish and again a human-like you would chase for the four magical stones" she told.

"What are the four magical stones?" I asked the witch.

"To turn everyone back to humans and destroy the evil spirit forever you need to get the 4 magical stones.

FIRE, WATER, EARTH, AND THUNDER." she told.

"George had managed to get 3 of them but he failed to get the 4th one, the Thunderstone as it's very difficult to achieve." She revealed.

"Then how did he manage to defeat the Rythom with just 3 stones?" I asked.

"At that time my powers were strong so we both together defeated the Rythom but as we didn't have the Thunderstone we couldn't finish him forever. After the battle, the stones returned to their original places," she told the entire story.

Now I understood the entire past of this town and about my Grandfather.

"Where are those 4 magical stones?" I asked.

"The firestone lies on top of an active volcano which is 5000ft tall and 500ft wide, even the mightiest of the eagles are afraid to go near the top"

"The water stone lies in between the middle of the lake which is surrounded by innumerable alligators."

"The earth stone is kept inside a cave, which is not less than an Everlong maze."

"And the Thunderstone rotates on top of a giant wind storm which rotates so fast that sometimes you can't even see it " she announced.

"Do I have to do it all by myself?" I blurted.

"Even if I come with you, it won't do any good to you as my powers have exhausted," she replied.

"So where is the active Volcano, the lake with alligators, the endless cave, and the storm?" I asked.

She handed me a map of the 4 stones. I looked at the map inquisitively, It was only guiding the way to reach the Volcano.

In anticipation, I asked her, "why is it only showing the way to reach the Volcano? What about the other three places?"

She told, "They all lie one after the other, once you reach the Volcano you would be able to see the next destination. Likewise, once you achieve a stone you can use its powers to achieve the other stones or even for your safety."

I can't give you much support in your journey but I can do you a little favor." said the witch while looking up, raising her left arm and chanting a mantra.

Suddenly something appeared in her hands. What could it be? I asked myself.

"Here, take these three magical darts." she offered.

"What are these?" I asked curiously.

"There are the darts, each one of them has a different power. But they can only be used once," she warned.

One of the darts had a sign of fire, another had a sign of water and the last one had a sign of a leaf.

"The dart with a fire sign will help you generate flames for some time."

"The dart with a water sign will help you control the movement of water for some time."

"And The dart with a leaf sign will help you control the movement of trees and their stems," she told.

With my mouth wide open, I thought to myself in shock, 'if that's a little help from her, then what could she do if she had her powers!'

I took the darts, they were to be inserted in my hand! she told me that whenever I would move my hand forward and shout 'fire', 'water' or 'leaf' they will become active and launch immediately whichever dart I call out.

"So cool! I feel like a superhero!" I exclaimed in joy.

"You have to get all the stones and then reach back to me before 7 days," she warned.

"What's after 7 days?" I asked in curiosity.

"After 7 days the creatures would permanently be turned into what they are now! after 7 days you can't transform them back to humans," she told.

I kept her warning in my mind and when I was about to leave, she gave me a pill and said, "After having this magical pill you wouldn't feel hungry for 7 consecutive days!"

I swallowed the pill right at that moment.

I thanked her for her hospitality. I had installed the darts in my hand, it didn't do any harm while inserting them. They just themselves went in and felt as if my hands had absorbed them easily.

I moved out of the witch's cave, with my pistol and the map.

"

CHAPTER FOUR

THE RED GIANT'S ANGER!

After leaving the cave, I analyzed the map thoroughly and found that the Volcano wasn't very far from my location. I started moving through the woods towards the Volcano. The way was really thorny and there were bushes all over, looked like I was going in a denser part of the woods.

After walking for six or seven consecutive hours, I could finally see the volcano!

It looked like a red hot giant! I had never seen a volcano before that too an active one. it looked as if it was just about to explode. As I went closer and closer, I could even hear some rumbling sounds that came from the volcano.

I tried to be as confident and brave as I could throughout the way, I again started waking until I had finally reached the volcano. It looked around 5000 feet tall just as the witch told.

I took some rest and started thinking of a plan to go on top of the Volcano without being burned. I couldn't handle the heat of the red giant, I needed a medium by which I could climb it.

It started turning dark, the moon was illuminating the sky. I decided to wait till the morning to execute my plan. I gathered some woods to lit up a fire and give myself some warmth.

I decided to sleep on top of a big flat rock while using my backpack as a pillow. I was staring at my pendant and thinking about my parents and Larra who had been overpowered by evil forces. I was also really worried about Jordy as he is still missing. I could try my level best to turn my parents and the entire town back to humans but how would I find Jordy? I slept while questioning myself.

The sun's rays woke me up. It was a bright morning. I yawned and looked around anxiously. I could see some wild monkeys playing on the branches of the pine trees.

Wait a minute? ahh, trees! I had got an amazing plan. The darts! the leaf dart! it could help me get to the top. I went near the pine trees, I moved my hand forward towards the trees and screamed, "Leaf!".

The dart immediately launched itself without any delay, it looked pure golden as It went towards the trees and burst into a mist that covered at least a thousand trees!

I thought about what I wanted to do, and it started happening! the trees began to combine their branches, making them like look a single rope, and quickly moved them towards the volcano's top. I quickly grabbed the rope, held the dry and hard stems tightly in both of my hands, and then with the flow of the rope went up to the Volcano's top. That speed was quite fast. I was really scared but also excited at the same time as I was swinging in the air.

"If I didn't hold the rope tight then I would surely fall and end up dying without even achieving a single stone!"

I was also trying to distance myself while swinging from touching the Volcano as It was extremely hot and filled with lava.

Soon I reached the Volcano's top, the air there was really warm, it was burning my skin. I tried to find the Fire Stone, and to my surprise, it was hanging in the air on top of the volcano. It was a bright red stone that was shining and looked very beautiful and shiny in appearance.

I made a bridge to the stone with the help of the stems and started swinging and moving forward on it slowly. Still, I could feel my skin burning, it felt really warm there. I wanted to get back as soon as I could.

I somehow managed to reach the stone, grabbed it tightly in my hand, and started to go back. But was it that easy?

As I was returning, the volcano produced a loud noise and the lava below me started raising!

Is it about to erupt! I asked myself. I ran towards the side and thought of making a safe slide from the branches with the help of the stems.

The trees made a straight broad slide to the base. I looked back and I could see the lava had already reached the top! I quickly ran towards the slide, jumped, and started sliding straight to the base. As I was sliding down, I could see lava flowing down the volcano and coming towards me. I raised my legs for getting a faster acceleration. In a matter of seconds, I had reached the base. The branch slide had ended but I still moved with the flow, in the air! I experienced a crash landing and felt straight on my back hitting the ground. "Ouchh!"

Luckily the stone was intact, I looked up and saw the lava coming towards me with a great speed, I started running towards the dense forest to escape myself from the lava. But after running for so much time I became extremely exhausted because of which my speed slowed down and the speed of lava surpassed me but in a different direction.

I thought I am gonna die but to my surprise, it couldn't harm me! "Was it because of the firestone?" I realized.

After two miles of running and crawling, I had finally escaped from the lava. Luckily, it wasn't a big eruption that could have lasted 30 miles far.

I took the firestone from my pocket, it was shining brightly. Was the Fire stone saving me from being burnt! I thought.

Ultimately it was the firestone so maybe it could save me or let me control fire or lava! I believed.

I was extremely exhausted, I took a short nap to regain my energy and strength. I slept for an hour or so but then I woke up because of the warm winds blowing my soul away. I realized that It was afternoon. I took the map out of my backpack and looked at it.

Now I could see the way to the Water stone! It was located in the middle of a lake, A alligator's picture was drawn on the map. I without thinking much started moving towards the lake. I was five miles away from the lake, I started moving towards it through the dense forest.

The way to the lake seemed quite calm and pleasant, there were white and red flower bushes which seemed way too beautiful. I even plucked some flowers for Larra and wrapped them from dead stems to make it look like a bouquet, in the hope of gifting her those flowers once she turns back to human.

I put the flower bouquet in my backpack and start heading toward the lake.

It had turned dark, I decided to sleep on top of a wide branch of a tree as the lake was nearby and it had many alligators who would be roaming on the shores of the lake.

I lay on the wide branch, thinking about my parents. "Would I be able to defeat the Rythom?" I asked to myself. "I at least want to see my untransformed parents for the last time if I die" I prayed to god.

I was also missing Jordy, I will again ask the witch if he's safe once again when I return to her. I thought.

I slept while crying and missing them with tears in my eyes and anxiousness in my mind.

CHAPTER FIVE

THE WATER SPLASH!

I opened my eyes as the bright rays of sunlight fell on my face, I got ready for the upcoming challenges.

"Today, I have to get the 2nd stone anyhow!"

I slowly and steadily started moving towards the lake with my eyes wide open and fully concentrated. I had reached its shore, I could see three alligators having a sunbath in the sand. I climbed on a tree to have a better look at the alligators in and out of the lake.

The water stone was in the middle of the black watered lake and several alligators were revolving around it as if they were there to protect it.

"I couldn't just walk forward and get the water stone," I analyzed.

If I had the leaf dart then again I would have gone through the air through the stems but this time I only had my pistol, the fire dart, and the water dart.

"Water dart can control water movement." hmm.. I tried to think of a plan.

"Could the firestone help me?" I thought about what the witch told me.

"What powers does the firestone has?" I questioned myself.

I decided to give it a try, I hang my backpack on a branch of a tree.

I took the firestone and withholding it, I tried to use it. I rubbed it and moved my hands forward toward one of the alligators.

To my surprise, the firestone produced a fireball in my hand! which didn't burn me. I stretched my hand and shot it towards the alligators. ***The fireball went at a speed of light and burnt three of them at once!***

With my mouth wide open I looked at the firestone. It was again shining as it was shining earlier. Now I had realized what its actual power was and how could I use it.

I moved my hand closer to my face and kissed the firestone for its extraordinary powers and started embracing it, but while embracing it I was slowly losing my senses. Seemed as if it was hypnotizing me! my eyes grew red and I jumped off the tree. All the alligators came out of the lake and aggressively approached me but I burnt every single one with the fire which was running inside my body and making me feel furious and herculean.

I burnt at least a hundred alligators! As time passed the fire inside me started vanishing. Slowly my anger abated and I couldn't believe that I could possess so much power within me that I could kill hundreds of alligators just with one of the four stones. I wondered if the firestone alone is so powerful then how invincible would I become when I would get the power of all the stones.

I started swimming towards the water stone but something huge came out of the water. ***IT WAS A HIPPOPOTAMUS!*** *I realized that the witch didn't tell me much about the dangers that I had to go through.*

I didn't even expect that there could be a hippopotamus in this lake, it started coming towards me. I tried to use the firestone but it didn't work maybe because my hands were all wet. I recalled the fact that fire is useless when it comes in contact with the water.

Only the water dart could save my life, I launched it towards the hippo and like the leaf dart, it too burst and formed like a mist. It had hit the hippo with a great impact, I thought to throw the hippo out of the lake, and with the thrust of water, it happened!

the water applied so much pressure on him that he literally flew in the air. I without any delay went to get the water stone. It was shining like a star, it was azure in color.

I grabbed it in my hands and thought to get to the shore safely, Now I knew how to use the stones now, I shook the stone inside the black water of the lake, Firstly it became clear and then It slowly started freezing.

The water converted into ice! the whole lake got frozen except for the part in which I was. Now I could easily walk on the ice and go away from the lake to a safe place.

I walked carefully to the side, holding fire and the water stone in my hands.

"I DID IT! now I also have the 2nd stone!" I shouted in excitement.

I was proud of myself, I had achieved 2 stones in just 2 days! I still had 5 days left to achieve all four and return to the witch.

OVERPOWERED!

I searched my backpack and took out the map as soon as I found it, Now I could see the way to the Earthstone. But I couldn't understand why a snake symbol was drawn beside the Earthstone on the map.

"What does this snake signify?" I asked myself in suspicion.

The caves were really far off, approximately 30 miles away and it would take me around 2 days to reach there. *I started moving towards the cave.*

The way seemed quite calm and composed as I could hear peacocks squawking and a lot of a wide variety of plants and flowers.

It soon turned afternoon, the sun was on top of my head. I found a small clean water pond, I washed my face and legs as they were dirty because of the black-watered lake. After refreshing myself, I changed my clothes with the ones I had kept. I took out the pistol from my backpack, held it in my hand, and again started moving towards the cave. The way was covered with dense forest, I came across many dears, rabbits, and boars. I had even seen two bears but I didn't let myself be seen by those two beasts. Luckily, I didn't came across any tiger or a jaguar. As a nature lover and an adventure-loving boy, This experience seemed exciting.

I kept moving until it was Evening, I decided to take a short nap under a tree, On top of the soft green grass bed. I had fallen asleep as soon as I laid there, it was really comfortable. As soon as I was about to go into a deep sleep, I felt, something huge felt on my stomach! I opened my eyes in fear.

IT WAS A DAMN MONKEY! He jumped off the tree and landed on my stomach. He wanted to trouble me which could be seen by his body language. I stood up, As soon as I could do something, A branch hit me hard on my head, I looked back. There were abound monkeys there, they all were finding me alien to the place. some of them tried to take away my backpack! I became furious, I took out the firestone from my pocket and targetted the monkeys with it to scare them away by some fire.

But as soon as I could even think of something, it released a fireball when I didn't even want it to. Just by the one fireball, hundreds of trees caught fire at once! all the monkeys trembled and started swinging on tree branches in terror to escape.

But I never intended to burn the forest! I got really afraid and shocked. Thousands of trees were on fire and it was because of my carelessness. I was really ashamed of myself, I had to do something to save the forest!

I tried to think of something but due to panic, I wasn't able to pacify myself. Suddenly, I thought of the Waterstone. I took it out from my pocket, holding it tightly in my hand, and lifted it up in the sky, trying if could bring some rain. A blue beam of light went up in the sky from the water stone, soon the black clouds covered the forest and it actually rained and extinguished the fire which turned the forest back into its normal state. When the fire had disappeared completely, I again lifted my arm. Again the blue beam of light went up in the sky and stopped the rain. Some trees had burnt completely and the others had been affected a little.

Being a nature lover, I felt even more disappointed and guilty about my decision of using firestone for such a meager situation. In remorse, I decided to plant trees once I get back home. I had realized that the stones were really powerful, I had to think twice before doing anything silly.

It was already night, But I continued my journey, I took the flashlight from my backpack which I had kept and didn't use till now. As I was moving, Cold winds were blowing me away. The temperature was really low. After some time when I just couldn't bear the cold winds, I decided to sit near a tree and give myself some warmth. I gathered some wood sticks and I lit up a fire.

I started warming my body. my legs were frozen, I couldn't feel them. I was shivering but slowly with time and heat, I could feel normal and gather the motivation to move forward again.

After some time of getting warmth, I again started moving forward in the chilled atmosphere of the woods. I was moving slowly to save more energy, Soon I had covered more than half of the way to the caves.

It turned morning but my legs didn't stop. I had decided to reach the caves in one go!

I had never felt that kind of motivation and enthusiasm which I felt that day. I wondered if I could teleport myself to the cave and save my energy but that wasn't possible. I kept moving, slowly but I didn't stop. The way seemed like a slope. I kept walking and walking, I didn't know when it turned afternoon and when did it turn to night. I just kept moving slowly without stopping.

It was night, Suddenly a group of fireflies surrounded me. The scene was beautiful, I felt like I was still in a magical world of untold life-threatening adventures. As soon as the fireflies went behind, I saw a huge mountain-sized rock. It had an entrance of a cave at its base.

"Have I reached the cave!?"I exclaimed in high spirits. I was so tired that I fainted near the entrance of the cave.

I was so sleepy and tired that I didn't even realize that it wasn't safe near the cave. It had turned midnight, I felt like someone was holding my body tightly.

I woke up, **IT WAS A PYTHON**! *it was slowly covering my entire body. I couldn't move my hands! the python had reached to my neck and was just about to bite me.*

What would the witch think of me? The new savior of the town died because of a snake- sting? NO!

I without thinking much, closed my eyes and started rolling my body towards the cave with the python. I stopped after I had reached the entrance of the cave. The Python seemed restless and I quickly ran away.

"Hasshh" I had saved myself.

I decided to go into the cave and return with the earth stone before tomorrow morning.

I took some dry woods, combined them, and made a firetorch with help of the firestone.

CHAPTER SEVEN

HALF DEAD!

As I moved deeper and deeper, I could see many bats who were hustling inside of the cave. I quickly ran forward so that they don't trouble me. As I kept moving, The cave became darker and gigantic. After some time I ended up reaching the center of the cave. There were 6 different ways which headed to different destinations.

I scratched my head, as I was so confused. "Where should I go?" I asked myself.

I tried guessing, I went in the one which was in front of me, the middle one. leaving behind the others. I kept moving in the cave but it was becoming really difficult to breathe! I took some rest and again started walking. After an hour of continuously walking, I thought I would soon reach the stone but to my surprise, I ended up reaching the same place from where I had started!

"God damn! This cave is a maze!" I cried out in anger, I was really tired as I didn't sleep much and now I couldn't even breathe properly.

"I can't walk more, my legs are paining!" I screamed in pain.

Suddenly, an idea came from within me, I didn't know if it would work but I had to try it once. If I had guessed it right, 5 out of 6 ways came back to where they all started. That meant if water is allowed to pass through all the ways and it reaches back here then the way would be incorrect. But I tried to do the same with fire, as I didn't want a cyclone in the caves.

I took out the firestone, filled my hands with flames, and with full power threw them in every direction one by one.

5 of them returned, but one didn't!

It was the 4th path! The one in the right direction. I started running as I had to get the earth stone as soon as I could.

As I moved inside the 4th path, it became even more difficult to breathe. At first, the passage seemed quite normal but after some time the unusual things came into sight! I ended up reaching a deep trench, upon which an old rope was in a very poor condition was tied up from my to the other end, It was acting like a bridge upon a valley. As I went closer and closer I kept feeling warmer. When I reached the rope, I sneaked down.

I became terrified and I started shivering even though it was warm there. As there was molten magma flowing down the trench, It had made the air over it so warm that I even had some skin burns by just being in contact with the air above.

"Nooo! I Can't do this..." A sense of fear arose within me. The rope on which I was supposed to take support was in such a bad condition that it could break by a slight jerk. But, I had no other choice except for moving ahead by holding the rope.

I took some long breaths and jumped off the cliff gently by holding the rope tightly in my hands. I was feeling so warm that I felt like a roasted chicken. I was sweating badly, I kept moving ahead slowly but the fear inside me increased even more.

Now was the point, I was swinging mid-air holding the rope. This was the hottest part, I started getting anxious and my grip became weak. One of my hands had already lost contact with the rope, I was swinging on top of the magma with only one hand support. My eyes were so irritated that I had tears flowing from them which made my sight blurry. *I felt like I was **half-dead!***

I was extremely exhausted, I just couldn't take it anymore. My hand was slowly losing its grip, it had lost all its energy. Hushh! my hand slipped and I started going into the magma.

I was falling slowly into the magma, I was feeling like I was about to die. I had lost all my hopes to return back and all I felt was guilt for not being able to save my family, and the town.

> *"I'M SORRY EVERYONE*
> *I'M SORRY DAD,*
> *I WASN'T A GOOD SON.*
> *I'M SORRY MOM,*
> *I COULDN'T SEE YOU AGAIN.*
> *I'M SORRY LARRA,*
> *YOUR BROTHER IS A LOOSER*
> *I'M SORRY JORDY,*
> *I COULDN'T FIND YOU.*
> *AND I'M SORRY GRANDPA,*
> *I WASN'T AS BRAVE AS YOU.*
> *I'M SORRY,*
> *EVERYONE."*

I thought I was dead but then I don't know how but I opened my eyes, and I found myself in a different dimension. Blue flames all over my body, Looked like some magic kept me alive.

My body felt numb. I couldn't feel myself, I couldn't move an inch! Suddenly, A bright golden light illuminated the place. Ahh! it's so bright!

An old man with a stick appeared in front of me. We were swinging in the air, something sort of a vacuum, wherein everything was hidden in complete darkness except for the golden aura. Surprisingly the old man looked quite familiar.

He began to speak:

""Dear Grandson,
I had left this locket for you to make it easier for you to repeat the history, my dear.
I was aware of how the need of a new saviour would arise after I'd die,
Thats why I had stored some of the most powerful powers of those stones in this locket.
It will help you defeat the Rythom.
You will always find me with you if you have this locket with you,
I feel guilty to not be with you when you'd be hearing this,
thats how nature is, my dear.
We can't go against what the nature has decided.
One who takes birth has to die.
I'm sure you would be a brave boy,
Remember, only you can defeat the Rythom.
You'll get strength whenever you'll feel the energy of this locket.
Now go and do what you're destined to do!
Jake, my dear."

Wait? couldn't he see me? Was this some sort of a replica or a message that he had left for me long back? that too is all in this locket? I became really emotional and confused.

I slowly came back to my senses and once again I opened my eyes, I found myself lying on the other end of the cliff. Was this a dream?

I looked back but to my surprise, the rope was broken and my locket was immensely shining. Does that mean that it was all real? Does this locket have so many powers stored within it that it saved me from dying? It surely was a mystery.

"I have no time to think about this!" I gotta hurry up and get the stone. I again started moving forward, the way was really narrow and it was only getting harder to breathe.

After some time of crawling, I could finally see a huge opening that surely led to a place that was way bigger than the way I was crawling into. I quickly got out of there and entered the opening, The scene which I saw after getting there was really unexpected.

The place wasn't covered from the top, It had an open roof that was the blue sky along with gigantic roots or stems of some anonymous plants which went all the way up. Not only this! ahead of me was a 5 feet tall mountain of gold coins and jewelry. On top of it was the Earth Stone which was stably set into the air.

The Earth stone had an emerald color and was shining immensely, the sight of the gold mountain along with the Earth stone made it look really special and pleasant to the eyes.

What made me the happiest, was that I could just get out of the cave by climbing those stems, I didn't want to go all the way back from where I came, however, the rope was also broken which made it practically impossible.

I started walking towards the gold mountain, I thought that I would just take away the stone but as soon as I stepped onto the gold mountain, A bunch of snakes appeared out of nowhere!

"Ohh no! Wasn't that python enough?" As soon as I could do anything, Hundreds of them surrounded me from all sides. I became anxious, the only thing I could do was to use the powers of the Fire or the water stones. I took them out of my pocket and tried to form a fire tornado with the fire stone and a water tornado with the water stone. I started moving my hands in a circular motion in order to form the tornados. Even though they had trapped the snakes within them, more and more snakes were approaching me. They were literally countless and I couldn't move my hands that fast for more than a minute, I had to take the stone as soon as possible.

I started climbing the gold mountain with my hands rotating, I slowly and steadily kept moving forward but then came to a point where I had to grab the Earth stone but both of my hands were occupied and also tired.

I applied all of the force that I had within me and tried to push all of them as far as I could, As soon as I had stopped rotating my arms, I quickly groped for the Earth stone. I had successfully grasped it in my hand but as soon as I could see the position of the snakes, They all had already reached near me and some of them were about to bite me.

I was really scared, my arms were really tired and I couldn't find a way to get out of there with the help of those 2 stones, The only thing that could save me was the mysterious powers of the Earth stone.

I had no other option than to try using it, while holding it in my hand I pointed it towards the sky. For a second, nothing happened but then I surely witnessed something which I hadn't seen before.

An emerald-colored mist surrounded the place, all the snakes had suddenly fainted, I tried to escape while this was happening, I reached the corner to climb those gigantic roots, The Earth Stone was able to control their movement, And just as I thought they were moving according to my will. I lifted myself up with those thick stems and started going to the top. As I was going up, the snakes began to move, but they luckily couldn't climb up the cave.

After some time, I had finally reached the top which led me into a forest. *I shouted in joy, "I did it!".*

I kept lying there for some hours as I was really tired and stood early morning.

I had all the 3 stones, I was very near to my target. I looked down the hole, The caves had completely destroyed themselves, I wondered if they would be the same when these stones would return to their original places again.

I looked at the map, Now the way to the Thunderstone was visible. I started analyzing the position of the Thunderstone, but it wasn't constant!

As it was on top of an ever-lasting tornado, it wasn't at a particular place. It kept on moving randomly but as I had a magical map, I was able to see its present position.

I headed towards the location, luckily it wasn't so far away! I still had 2 days to reach the witch.

I started moving forward, the way to the tornado firstly seemed normal but tiring. It was all rocky, I had to climb many rocks so that I could go on top of them.

but after some time I could see the barren and abandoned parts of the woods.

"Is it because of the Tornado!?" I asked myself.

My great-grandfather held the three stones which I am holding right now, but he wasn't able to get the Thunderstone. It must be really difficult to get it!

It turned to night, The moon started showing off its beauty. I had almost made it to the tornado, the area near it seemed like a desert. I decided to wait there till tomorrow morning. I had to sleep on the sandy surface as it didn't have any trees or vegetation.

I looked at the moon with hope, "I AM COMING, MOM AND DAD! JUST WAIT SOME TIME MORE..."

The sky was completely illuminated with shiny stars, I tried to spot some constellations. I didn't see such a clear sky before. I just kept wondering about tomorrow and also the mysterious powers of these stones.

Earlier I could not sleep anywhere apart from my bed but now, because of the situation I was in, I could sleep anywhere. On the branches, sand, anywhere. I had developed a habit of sleeping anywhere now.

"I don't think I would be able to sleep on my cozy bed now." I smiled while thinking and fell asleep.

"*I was swirling inside the speedy tornado,*
my head ached like it was about to explode.
I had lost all the stones i had achieved.
I died.
**THD DEMONS SUCCEDED IN THEIR DEMONIC INTENTIONS..*"*

Aghast... I woke up sweating. I looked around in terror.

"Just a dream...hasshh" I took a sigh of relief.

"Such a horrible dream!" I checked my pocket for the stones, fortunately, they all were there.

"But what if I lost them? Then what will I do!" I hesitated.

I started moving forward without overthinking, I saw many small animals like foxes, snakes, lizards, and some Scorpios.

I kept moving for some time, soon the tornado was visible.

It wasn't a normal tornado, **IT WAS GIGANTIC!** and by that, I mean even greater than the volcano!

It was literally a Wind Giant!

It felt even more dangerous as I tried to go near it. Luckily I had chained pockets so I could keep the stones safe inside them.

I had reached near the tornado, having the earth stone held tightly in my hands and the others in my pockets. I had raged myself up by using the firestone so that I no longer feel any fear to face it.

CHAPTER EIGHT

PLEASE, LET ME TAKE IT!

It was trying to blow me away but I had kept myself grounded because of the Earthstone.

I began to test the powers which I had, I again felt the rage and the anger within me that I felt before while killing those alligators.

My eyes were brown but now they had turned green! I raised my arm toward the Wind Giant, A dark green beam of light quickly struck the Tornado. It kept on increasing its intensity, and the anger inside me grew even more.

I took out the firestone along with the water stone to provide support.

I used every stone's power together on the tornado, The tornado turned into a tri-color giant in appearance. Its bottom turned green, the middle turned blue, and the top turned red in color.

Now even the Tornado started backfiring, It started coming towards me!

I began to move backward slowly, the tornado was intact! I couldn't see any change in the Tornado's power.

I lowered my hands and started running away.

But I wasn't successful, the tornado's force was so strong that it blew me away. I used the earth stone for a safe landing. "I had to think something else" I realized.

I again took all the stones and this time I aimed at the Tornado's very base.

It was really small, even smaller than me.

I with full rage and power applied all the powers altogether at its base. Still, the effect wasn't enough, I needed more power to slow it down.

Suddenly I remembered what my grandfather had told me, the locket! I concentrated on my locket while applying the powers of the three stones. And it worked! It too generated a beam of light, but it was a rainbow! it had a blend of the seven colors of the rainbow, and as soon as it struck the Wind Giant, a clear change in the tornado could be observed. It seemed as if the power of the locket was much more than that of these three stones combined.

It was working! the tornado began to slow down, now I could see the Thunderstone!

It was a black shiny-looking stone.

I just had the fire dart now, I launched it towards the Storm.

I had used everything I had to get the 4th stone, the Tornado was the most powerful barrier I had seen till now in the whole journey.

It took me an hour to finish the Tornado completely.

The thunderstone began to come down slowly, I ran to grab it.

But as soon as I could get it, an arrow strikes my left leg. I fell to the ground, I look from where it had been launched. It was a tribal group, it seemed like they protected the Thunderstorm.

I couldn't kill any human! I thought. They came near me, I requested them to let me take the Thunderstorm.

"**Please let me take it**, I need it to defeat the Rythom." I cried.

They started looking at each other, they lifted me on a log and took me somewhere.

My leg was bleeding and I had fainted.

I didn't know if I would be able to get the Thunderstone and reach the witch in time.

After some time, I opened my eyes.

"Where am I?" I asked.

"You are in our village." An old man told.

"Why you carried me here? I am on a very important mission right now, I don't have time to waste" I asked in a high pitch.

"Give me the thunderstone!" I exclaimed.

"You have to help us otherwise we would not hand over to you your stones," they said.

Stones!? I checked my pockets, and none of the stones were there!

"Give me my stones back please!" I screamed.

"But for that, you have to help us" He again highlighted.

"What help do you want from me?" I asked.

"You have to defeat the Luro" he announced.

I sat up, my leg wasn't paining anymore. Looked like they have medicated it.

"Who is this Luro now?" I asked in suspicion.

"He is a Monster! every day he comes here and takes someone or the other for his meal.

"Earlier we were about four thousand tribals but now only 12 people are left to be taken." he cried.

"Has he eaten everyone!?" I asked in anger.

"Not everyone, he eats one person every day. He has captured the rest," he cried.

"Ok! tell me where he lives, and I will bring your people back safe and sound. I agreed.

They gave me my stones except for the Thunderstone.

"We will hand over to you the Thunderstone once you bring our people back," The old man said.

"It would have been easier if you would give me the Thunderstone but never mind. I'll defeat Luro with these stones." I announced.

I started moving towards the location they told me to go on. I could see a gigantic cage that was kept outside of a cave.

Hundreds of tribal people which included small children, women, and old people were kept inside it.

I felt really sad for them, I was thankful to God that he had granted me an opportunity to help them.

"Luro! Come out you evil! Show me what you got!" I shouted at the top of my voice.

Suddenly the ground began to shake, as a 40 feet tall monster came out of the cave. He was fully black in color, he wore some ornaments made from human bones. His eyes were red in anger and by his tummy, it felt like he could accommodate at least a thousand people within him.

"Oops, I didn't expect that." I thought to myself in regret.

"L..L..Leave these people!" I tried to shout while looking at his monstrous structure.

He began to come towards me, I took out the firestone and tried to burn him intact.

But, to my surprise, it didn't work!

The monster wasn't weak, I took out all the stones I had and together tried to capture it.

With the Earth stone, I created a huge hole inside the ground below Luro's legs. He felt and tried to lift himself to the ground but as soon as he could do something, I burnt his hands, he completely felt inside the deep hole.

I didn't stop here, I closed the hole and kept a huge rock on top of the hole with the help of the Earth stone so that he wouldn't come again. He was buried alive! That's what he deserves.

I opened the cage and released the tribal people.

They all were happy to be free again, I took them back to their Tribe.

The old man cried in joy after seeing his family again. They all were crying and celebrating their freedom. I too felt good for being able to help them.

"Now can I have the Thunderstone?" I asked the old man in a polite voice.

"But only when you stay here at Night and celebrate with us." said the old man.

Although I had to reach the witch tomorrow, I agreed as I couldn't say no after seeing his joyous face.

At Night they lit a huge campfire, they were dancing near it and sang a particular song over and over. They were also making food inside large pots.

I felt like I had traveled to the ancient era.

After some time the old man called me and he awarded me the Thunderstorm in front of everybody while they clapped and cheered for me.

I was given a personal hut to spend the night, I slept in peace after many days and eagerly waited for tomorrow morning.

CHAPTER NINE

MERGE EM ALL!

It turned morning, I woke up in high spirits for the battle,
I met the old man before going from the village.
"Thank you for helping us," he said.
"That was my duty, Now I have to travel a long journey and reach the witch before it's too late," I said.
"You don't need to walk all the way back!" he exclaimed.
"Why?" I asked curiously.
"Don't you know the superpowers of the Thunderstone?" he asked.
"Ahh actually I don't," I hesitated.
"Let me tell you then-"
THE THUNDERSTORM CAN TELEPORT YOU FROM ONE PLACE TO ANOTHER AT THE SPEED OF LIGHTNING!
IT CAN MAKE YOU FLY IN THE SKY JUST LIKE CLOUDS.
AND LASTLY, IT CAN RELEASE IMMENSE LIGHTNING WHICH CAN END ANYONE AND ANYTHING"
I almost fainted, I didn't know it was that powerful!
Some days back I had been thinking that Teleportation isn't possible but today, I myself could experience it.

"Thank You for the information" I thanked the old man.

Although I could teleport myself, I chose to experience flying.

First I went outside their village then I took out the Thunderstone, held it tightly, and pointed it towards the sky. I started flying like a superhero! I could easily control myself while flying. I quickly flew towards the witch's cave.

It hardly took me an hour to reach the witch's cave.

I entered her cave, she was making a portion, she saw me and exclaimed in joy, "WELCOME! I WAS WAITING FOR YOU. DID YOU GET ALL THE FOUR STONES?" she asked.

I showed her all the 4 stones with a smile on my face.

"That's the spirit! Great work, you are the first person who got all the 4 stones" she plauded.

"Thank You, dear Witch, but it wasn't possible without you and your magical darts." I smiled.

"Now let's merge them!" she ordered.

"How will we?" I asked in curiosity.

She took all the four stones and kept them together on a rock. She poured some drops of the portion which she had made on each one of them.

The stones began to move, they slowly came closer and they merged.

A bright light illuminated the cave, I couldn't open my eyes!

When the light became dim, I slowly opened my eyes. They had formed one single stone which seemed adorable. It was pure white in color.

The witch took the stone and rubbed it on my chest. It slowly went inside!

I suddenly felt like I had gained a lot of energy and strength. I felt like I could win this entire world.

"Now these four powerful stones have merged and mixed with your blood, now nobody knows what kind of power combination would they form together, because they weren't merged till now" she announced.

I asked her, "So what do we have to do now?"

"Now you have to go back to Vennington, The Rythom will only appear at night, in the morning his powers are diminished, Just like a vampire. But he is becoming powerful day by day.

Tonight, he'll have the deadliest powers he ever had. " She warned.

"Aren't you coming with me?" I asked in fear.

"I wouldn't come with you but I will constantly keep an eye on your battle, if I feel that you need me then I will surely try to help you." She insisted.

"But how will I now use the power of these stones, since they have merged and are within me?" I asked in confusion.

"You just have to think, now it's even easier for you to use the power of these stones." she clarified.

I went out of the witch's cave and I started flying towards Vennington at a great speed.

CHAPTER TEN

THE INVINCIBLE LOVE!

I quickly flew over the woods, now I could see the town. The town was covered in dark green clouds, the clouds were only on top of the town.

First of all, I went to see the condition of my house. No one was there outside the house, our garden which my mom had kept so well-maintained was all barren. Every single plant had died. I went to see the pond, every aquatic animal had died. I felt really sad and worried about Vennington's situation.

I went inside my house, everything seemed creepy. The walls were scratched, There was some blood on the floor and complete darkness.

I tried to switch on the lights but the switchboard had been taken out and broken. I took a fireball in my hands and tried to see.

Everything was out of its place, and most of the things were broken along with my heart.

I moved to the 2nd floor, to my room.

As soon as I opened the door, suddenly something hit me hard in the face!

I fell to the floor and saw up, it was my dad! He had turned completely into a scary creature that just wanted to devour human blood.

Tears rolled down my eyes, "DAD! I AM YOUR SON JAKE, DON'T YOU REMEMBER ME!?" I cried.

He didn't seem to even listen to me, He again tried to attack me but I used my powers and tried if I could turn him back into a human.

A pink color beam was released from my hands, it hit him straight in the heart.

I was worried, I just wanted to stop him. I didn't intend to hurt him.

The pink beam seemed really beautiful, it kept going in his heart and my dad fainted.

Slowly his creepy appearance began to change, and his long canines and nails began to vanish.

HE WAS TURNING BACK INTO A HUMAN!

I quickly went to him, lifted his head, and kept it on my lap. I was staring at him, his inhuman face began to turn back to normal. Tears rolled down my eyes, but this time the tears were of happiness.

Dad had completely turned into a human, I went and got him some water.

I sprinkled some water droplets on his face to wake him up.

He slowly opened his eyes and lifted his head.

"Ahgh, Where am I? My head's about to explode from pain."

"Dad! Are you alright?" I asked while crying.

"Jake!" he hugged me.

"I missed you, dad, I really missed you.." I cried.

"I don't remember, a purple mist was turning everyone into horrible spooky creatures. I tried to escape but I too turned into something." He told.

"It's a pleasure to see you again my son.." he too cried.

"Dad, we need to save the entire town! It's just you who I have managed to turn back to human." I informed him and also told him about my entire journey.

He patted my back and complimented me on my bravery, **"I' AM PROUD OF YOU JAKE".**

"Do you know where are mom and Larra?" I asked dad.

He tried to remember but he just couldn't.

I requested him to stay home and look after the damage till I turn everyone back into humans.

I went outside to search for more creatures so that I could turn them back into humans.

The creatures were all around the town, I had to think of a plan to transform all of them at once.

The only plan which came to my mind was-

"Let's repeat the history, The purple mist was responsible for turning everyone monstrous, now the pink mist will turn everyone back to human." I thought inside my head.

I flew to the town hall, I scratched my hand until it started bleeding, I then shouted at top of my voice "MONSTERS! COME OUT IF YOU WANT SOME HUMAN BLOOD!" I played a trick to gather them.

Soon, all the creatures began to come out and gather at the town hall, I concentrated and started moving my hands like a fan, in a circular motion slowly and steadily.

And after some time I applied all of my energy up in the sky. The pink beam went up high in the sky and burst into pink mist.

It splashed and fell on the creatures. Slowly every creature fainted and started becoming a human.

I again used my powers to bring some rain and wake up everyone.

Every creature had turned back to the human they actually were and they all woke up and saw me like I was an alien. Cause, obviously they didn't see someone flying like that up in the sky before.

"Jake!" A voice reached my ears, it was my mom! I quickly landed and hugged her.

"I missed you mom!" I cried.

Larra my sister too came from behind and hugged me.

Everyone was looking for their family and crying because of reuniting again.

I felt really blessed and motivated as God had chosen me for this noble cause. Now I just had to defeat the Rythom who would return in the dark.

Everyone went to their houses, I took mom and Larra back home.

After seeing Dad, Mom and Larra couldn't stop their tears. We all hugged each other and felt blessed that we were together again.

But my work wasn't over.

Mom and Larra asked about how did I manage to do this, I again explained to them the whole adventure which I had been through since a week.

They all cheered me up, It was Evening. "It's time for the battle," I announced.

CHAPTER ELEVEN

THE POWERPLAY!

"Can we help you in some way?" asked Larra.

"Hmm.." I smiled and gave her the Bouquet I had made for her.

The flowers were dried because of no sunlight or water but still, they seemed quite beautiful.

"It's for you, I hope you will like it. " I tried to be kind.

"Once I end him, the first thing I will do is find Jordy," I murmured.

I flew away at the speed of a missile, I covered the sky with black clouds by using the powers of the Thunderstone and waited for the Rythom to appear.

After It turned to night, A small black hole appeared in the sky from which came the Rythom.

He was so black that I couldn't even see his face properly.

It said, "Hey kiddo, get ready for your doom"

"Sorry devil, but I wouldn't let you stay alive for long," I Shouted.

All the people were confined to their homes, watching and cheering me up from the windows.

The Rythom started his black magic, he threw several black flames on me but I destroyed all of them at once with a flash of strong lightning.

*Suddenly something sharp and huge hit me on my head from behind. I turned around, **It was an unusually bigger bat!** It was Rythom's pet.*

I tried to attack it but the Rythom from the front kept attacking me with his dark magic power balls. It really irritated me, I thought to again let the raged powers control me, I slowly let the anger of all the stones come inside of me till they both kept hitting me. The bat with his claws and the Rythom with his magic.

Soon my eyes turned red in anger, the sky began to terrify people. Strong bolts of lightning illuminated the dark sky. I controlled all of them and together released them on the Rythom, he felt on the ground. Till I froze the bat in ice with my water stone powers.

It too felt on the ground. I again concentrated on the Rythom, but now he wasn't visible.

He came from behind me and kicked me very hard, I went to the other opposite side by its force. I didn't want to stretch this battle for long. I just wanted to finish him as soon as I could.

We were face to face once again, We both kept attacking each other with our dangerous powers. I gathered all the lightning from the sky in my hand and struck it on him with my full power.

He too defended himself by making a small black hole that sucked all the lightning inside it.

I without any delay did another attack, I lifted up two very huge rocks with the power of the Earthstone and tried to smash him between them.

But he too was powerful, he stopped both the rocks from his hands, turned them black, and backfired them on me. I destroyed them with my fire powers.

The battle lasted the entire night, no one was willing to give up. The battle seemed to be ever-lasting, Neither I nor the Rythom stopped attacking each other.

I even tried to create a lava wave and a tornado in the air to destroy him, but he survived it. Although he seemed to be injured he was still fighting.

Soon it turned 12 AM in the morning, He began to cruelly laugh at me as now his powers were at their peak.

But I just gave a smile in return which somewhere hit him in his ego. I flew at the speed of light towards him and pushed him with so much force that he fell on the town statue and broke it, he felt so forcefully that it had created a hole in the ground even after destroying the statue.

I didn't stop, I had all the anger and rage inside of me. I with both hands released lava on him while he was lying in the hole.

"Ahhhhh!! " He began to scream in pain.

I was so deeply hurt by what he had done that blood tears rolled down my eyes, I wanted to listen to his painful screams. I just didn't want to simply end him like that.

He had created a shield and again flew up in the dark sky, he multiplied himself into hundreds of clones. Some attacked me while some started attacking people's houses.

I was being attacked from every side, I had made a shield around me which was saving me.

I again took the help of the lightning and threw it on all the clones of the Rythom.

Every clone of him vanished but I still couldn't see the real Rythom.

"Where did he go!?" I asked myself.

Then suddenly I realized something, I quickly flew to my house.

There he was in the air! He had captured Larra and with her support he tried to escape from me as he knew he couldn't win and I wouldn't attack my sister.

"Leave my sister you coward!" I screamed.

He started attacking me, but I could only save myself. I couldn't attack him because he had Larra lifted up in his hands.

"I had to do something before he escapes and again repeats the same with my town,"

I teleported myself, went to his back, and kicked him. He leaves Larra's hand and I quickly save her from falling and instruct her, "GO IN AND CLOSE THE WINDOWS! QUICK!"

The Rythom uses his black magic and ties me up tightly with black chains. I can't move!

The Rythom used his deadliest powers which he hadn't used for so many hours, for this moment.

He tries to control my mind!

"Let's finish this, kiddo," He says in a dreadful voice.

"That's what I am going to do," I reply with a monstrous smile while bending my head down.

"Aghhhhhhh!" I shouted for I was trying to wake up all of the powers I had. I activated the powers of my locket, The rainbow beam of light struck him. He seemed to be paralyzed.

I looked at the town clock tower, it was about to be morning. I completely paralyzed him in the air with the powers of the locket and then I remove all the dark clouds from the sky.

The sun's rays illuminated the sky, and the rays fell on Rythom. Seeing that terror in his eyes, gave me a really pleasant feeling.

He looked in a pathetic condition and while screaming in pain, broke into a million tiny pieces and evaporated.

I had won the battle, the fire of revenge in me had been extinguished by his dreadful doom.

THE AFTER EFFECT!

After the Rythom was defeated, the white stone came out of my body and divided itself into the four other stones, They went back to their original positions.

Everyone in the town came out of their houses, cheering for me.

My Mom, Dad, and Larra were crying, but those tears were for the victory of Good over Evil, The victory of humanity over the evils, and The victory of mine over Rythom.

The Rythom was destroyed but his bat wasn't, people asked me what to do with the bat.

"Let's keep it in the town Zoo!" I recommended.

The mayor agreed and called the zoo to take the bat with them and keep it in a separate cage at the zoo.

Immediately after that, I went to the woods to meet the witch in her cave but she wasn't there.

"Where could she be!?" I looked around.

Then I saw a piece of paper on top of a rock.

It was a note, which said:

*"**CONGRATULATIONS JAKE,***

I KNEW ONLY YOU COULD DO IT.
THE EVIL SPIRIT HAS BEEN DESTROYED
FOREVER,
NOW I TOO HAVE BEEN CALLED BACK TO
SERVE THE LORDS.
THE WITCH "

I was aback, Tears rolled down my eyes, the real savior of the town had left. The savior who had kept this town safe and sound for so many years was no more among us. I took the note with me and left her cave.

I tried to find Jordy near the cave but I couldn't, It turned evening but I wasn't in the mood to go home without Jordy. My mom and dad assured me that we would again come tomorrow and find him.

The next day, the Mayor of the Town came to our house to offer me something.

"Jake, we all have decided to make your statue in place of the one which was destroyed." He offered.

Mom, Dad, and Larra became excited and began to celebrate but, I wasn't in favour of this decision.

"Sorry sir, but I haven't done anything, It was someone else because of whom we were alive for so long," I said while looking up in the sky, thinking about the witch.

"Then whose statue should we make now!?" asked the Mayor's assistant.

"The real savior of the town, THE GOOD WITCH!" I recommended.

The Mayor agreed and he continued the work on the statue of the witch which was around twenty feet tall, I had made a sketch to tell the artists how she looked.

After some days the Mayor also arranged a prize ceremony to appreciate my efforts in protecting the town and gave me a medal.

I somehow went there ignoring my phobia, everyone started clapping and cheering when I went on the stage to claim my medal.

I took the mic from the Mayor and narrated the full story of my adventure in front of everyone.

"I want to dedicate this medal to the Good Witch as without her It was impossible," I ended the speech.

We came back home. But I still wasn't happy.

"Why are you sad, son?" asked my dad

"Everything's sorted but I couldn't find Jordy, Because of me he.." I cried.

"We will find him, don't worry." he insisted.

Suddenly a barking sound broke my ears, I recognized it! I quickly went outside to see if I was right.

I was right! It was Jordy! He seemed in a perfect condition.

I hugged him tight and cried. A note was stuck on his belt, I kept it in my pocket and went in.

In the evening, I sat at my desk. I remembered the note, I opened it.

THANK YOU FOR THE STATUE JAKE :)

I knew who it was, the witch must have found Jordy before leaving her body, and now she must be watching me from heaven, I believed.

After this adventure, no one called me a doofus anymore.